The Lion's Quest
for Freedom and Family

Sarah E. Ganesh

The Lion's Quest for Freedom and Family

Copyright © 2023 Sarah E. Ganesh

ISBN: 978-1-990330-47-6

editing, layout and design by
Saplings
a branch of One Thousand Trees
www.onethousandtrees.com

Contents

Acknowledgments

First I would like to thank the God of Abraham, Isaac, and Jacob for making this book possible. The morals of His Word inspires me in all aspects of my life. I would like to thank my dear mother Elizabeth and my father Vickram for bringing me into this world and for always challenging me to be better each day. Special thanks to my grandmother Chandrama and aunts Rebecca, Ann and Margaret who supported me through every step of this book. They are my greatest role models and feel like mothers to me. I would also like to thank my sister Victoria as well. She has been the greatest friend I could ever have. Thanks to my special cousin Neriyah who has always been there for me and journeyed with me through the ups and downs of life. I also want to thank my cute little cousin Isaac for his pleasant laughs and inspiration. Not forgetting my talented uncle David, thank you for always showing support for me and encouraging my writing and drawing talents from a young age. At last but not least, I thank my heavenly grandfather Harrichand whose steps I follow, in his love for God and enthusiasm for writing. I love you all!

Chapter 1

The Beginning

It was a sad, scary night at the North African National Park. A Barbary lion was cold heartedly killed by evil poachers. The park rangers were lucky enough to catch the poachers, but they were devastated because two lionesses and a never-before-seen rare black lion cub were now unprotected in the wilderness. Everyone wished they could go back in time to save the lion. He could have been saved but one small move resulted in the end of his life.

It all started when the pride was lying down on a flat rock surrounded by thick dry grass. There was Bomani, the pride leader and his mate Sitara, along with their cub Hairan, and Sitara's younger sister Deepa. Everyone was peacefully asleep except for Sitara, who was tiredly awake watching her cub. She looked at the midnight sky and slowly her eyes began to close. As she went to lay her head down, she heard a strange sound. Each second, it seemed to grow closer and closer. She saw bright lights shining through the grass. Bomani and Deepa suddenly woke up. They could hear the voices of men.

The pride was in grave danger. Sitara gently picked up Hairan with her mouth, and along with Deepa, they ran ahead speedily into the grass. Bomani decided he would lead the poachers away from them no matter what it would take.

But his plan did not work out. One of the poachers had already seen the mother with her rare and valuable cub. Sitara and Deepa were at the edge of the tall grass. They could either turn to the side and stay within the grass or run ahead into an open field. Each second, the poachers grew closer. Sitara could not think properly in such a stressful time. Confused, she ran ahead without thinking about the consequences.

Now, the men could see the lionesses even more easily. Bomani saw one of the poachers aiming their gun at Sitara. As the poacher prepared to pull the trigger, Bomani leaped from the tall grass into midair, blocking her. The gunshot pierced the silence of the night. Sitara heard the heavy thud of his body. She stopped for a moment as she stared at Bomani's body with tears in her eyes. She felt she wanted to remain there, but she had to save her sister and son. The poachers were more interested in her because of her cub.

Eventually, they reached a cliff, but they were surrounded. It seemed they would be caught, but they were able to dive off the cliff into the deep, dark waters below. The hunters turned around, thinking they were dead. But they were so wrong.

Surprisingly, the lionesses and Hairan survived the fall, safely landing in the middle of a baobab tree that was growing at the edge of the river. They climbed down, heavily panting. Deepa lay beside the river, struggling with fright and great fear while Sitara ran off with Hairan, leaving her."I have failed you," said Sitara sadly while nuzzling her son. With a heavy heart, Sitara moaned, alerting the creatures in the area of her presence.

Sitara heard a jackal howling. She carried Hairan, following the noise. She then found a female jackal with pups beside her. It was the same jackal she had saved from hyenas many years ago. "Take this cub and raise him as your own. Never tell him about me and his past. His name is Hairan," said Sitara as she placed him in front of her. Before the jackal could even reply, Sitara ran off. She began to run farther north, leaving the park. Through a hole in the fence on the borders of the park, she entered the wilderness.

A voice called out for her. It was her sister."Where are you going? Where is Hairan?" asked Deepa worriedly. Sitara ignored her as she continued to walk. Her sister knew that she was sad. She refused to back off and still went after her.

"Stop following me!"shouted Sitara.

"Are you just hurt that Bomani is dead?"asked her sister.

"Get out of here and leave me alone!"roared Sitara.

Deepa was shocked. Sitara had never said something so hurtful to her. She ran back, crying. Sitara immediately regretted what she had said. But it was too late. She ventured into the unknown, where life would be hard. Meanwhile, the jackal, whose name was Zahara, was staring outside and wondering why Sitara had given up her son and had looked so sad. All she knew was that she had to take care of Hairan, and she would do it to the best of her abilities.

She remembered the day Sitara had saved her. She was just a few months old when she got separated from her parents by a stampede. She wandered into the savannah, crying for her parents. But all it did was attract predators. As she walked through the dry grass, she noticed a group of eerie shadows. Creepy cackles came from all around. They came closer and closer. She then realized they were hyenas.

She had started to run away, but she wasn't fast enough. She was soon cornered by the watering hole. The hyenas growled loudly as they inched in. Suddenly, a deeper louder growl came from behind the hyenas. A big lioness was behind them. The group of five hyenas could've possibly taken her down. But then another younger lioness came, followed by a large male. The hyenas were scared. They had never seen a lion so gigantic. They scampered away in fear.

The lioness turned to her. Zahara was so frightened. Hyenas and now lions? Why were so many animals after her? She then closed her eyes as she whimpered. "I'm Sitara. This is my sister Deepa and mate Bomani. What is your name?" asked the big lioness kindly.

"I'm Zahara," the pup replied.

"Zahara, do you have any idea where your parents are? It's not safe to be out in the open like this. There are evil creatures who will eat young animals like pups," said Sitara.

"I got separated from my parents by a stampede. I can't find them," replied Zahara.

Sitara called out to Zahara's parents. They came immediately and hugged Zahara. They thanked Sitara and the lions so much for saving their daughter. The jackal family prepared to leave. Zahara went to Sitara and hugged her. "I promise I will repay you someday. I will always be indebted to you. If you hadn't come, I would've been dead!" Zahara said, crying.

Sitara gently nuzzled her as she said "Okay, but you should go to your parents now. It's getting late." Zahara went off, vowing to never forget the kindness the pride had showed her. It would leave a deep impression on her young mind forever.

Her thoughts were interrupted as slow and heavy footsteps came towards her. She looked into the distance to see her weary mate Jabari coming to the den. "The drought has driven prey farther north. If the rain doesn't come back soon, I'm afraid the pups won't make it," said Jabari. He then noticed an unfamiliar scent. "What's that strange scent?"asked Jabari. Zahara covered Hairan with her tail. Jabari asked, "What is that creature?"

"He's a lion cub," Zahara said worriedly.

"A black lion? Zahara, you know we can't take care of him. We can't even take care of our own pups. He's just an extra mouth to feed!"complained Jabari.

"No, this cub is my son. If you don't accept him, you'll have to leave," Zahara said angrily. She began to growl as Jabari finally agreed. But raising Hairan wouldn't be as hard as they expected. A few days later, the unexpected happened. Rain fell rapidly, flooding the land. Prey flourished and green grass started to appear. It was no longer desolate. Now, it would be a joyful time for all the animals, especially for Hairan and the jackals. They would get more food than they would need. As months passed, the young cub, along with the jackal pups, grew big and strong.

The pack was grateful for Hairan. He could take down big prey and scare away enemies. However, the pack was cautious of their surroundings and told Hairan he could not go out alone beyond their territory, since a human might see him. That was not the true reason why they didn't want him to venture out alone. Hairan had no knowledge that lions existed. He believed he was a jackal. As a cub, he questioned his appearance, but his mother told him that he was born unique. Sometimes Zahara and Jabari worried what would happen if he met a lion. They believed that if he found out about his past, he would leave the pack, but they knew they couldn't keep it a secret forever.

Five years later, Hairan and the jackals were now adults. Everything seemed to go well until something tragic happened. One day, the pack went to go hunt a gazelle. The pack planned to surround it while Jabari pounced on it. As he leaped, in midair, his head began to swing. He was barely able to cling onto the gazelle, and he fell down unconscious. The gazelle would have trampled him if Hairan wasn't there. The mighty lion chased the gazelle away from Jabari. It was just a mere example of how much Hairan cared for the jackals.

The pack helped Jabari walk home. As they laid him in the cave, they all were worried. Jabari had recently started to feel strange. He felt as if he did not have a long time to live. He was very old and realized it was time to give his place as the alpha to someone else. Most of his pups had already dispersed at the time, and only four chose to stay. He would have told them to start their own packs if it weren't for Zahara. She wouldn't be able to survive alone. He looked at their skills, leadership, and most of all their care. Only one was right to be the new alpha. It was Hairan. He was a skilled hunter, a strategist, and an excellent leader. The pack was overjoyed when Hairan was chosen to be the new alpha.

But one member wasn't pleased by Jabari's choice. The eldest pup, Musafa, was furious. He was supposed to be the heir, but now Hairan was chosen. Throughout his life, he always felt as if Hairan was the favorite of Jabari and Zahara. He had to get rid of the lion somehow. Soon, he came up with the perfect plan.

Chapter 2

The Shocking Truth

It was a calm night. Everyone was asleep in the den except for Hairan. He was lying down in the tall grass, watching the starry sky. He sighed as he continued to wonder why he felt something was missing in his life. Suddenly, he heard footsteps heading towards him. He got up instantly as he began to snarl. The creature turned out to be Musafa.

"What are you doing out here alone?"asked Musafa, cunningly grinning.

"Nothing. I just came out here to see the stars," said Hairan.

"I know something's troubling you. What is it?"asked Musafa.

"I just feel there's something more to my life. It just doesn't feel right," said Hairan.

"Well, maybe there is something more," said Musafa. Hairan turned to him, eagerly listening while he continued "What if your whole life has been a lie, and everything you knew and grew up with was just false?"

"What do you mean?"asked Hairan. Musafa laughed as he stared into a puddle, and then he said, "Look at me and you. Do we even have a slight resemblance? Just face it. You're not a jackal."

"No! My mom said I'm unique!"shouted Hairan.

Musafa went deeper as he said, "Mother and Father lied to you. Now, I'm going to tell you the truth. The real truth! You are a lion. You were given away by some lioness who didn't want you. My mother vowed she would never tell you about your past, but I will! You're a lion!"

Hairan stared at Musafa in shock as he slowly backed away shaking his head. "You're lying!" Hairan roared.

Musafa laughed wickedly as he said, "Why don't you ask the one you call Mother?"

Hairan realized it was the truth. He sprinted away with tears in his eyes. After a while, Hairan went into a cave to think about what had happened. He thought to himself, "I can't believe it. My entire life has been a dream that I just woke up from. All I've been taught is fake. What will I do?"He stared outside as an idea popped into his head. He would ask the Eagle of Wisdom about these "lions."He heard from the other animals that she knew all the secrets of the rainforest and would tell any creature what they wanted to know about the rainforest, for the price of a fish. Then he would be able to truly understand his past.

He hunted a fish from a nearby stream and went to Shimmering Falls, where the Eagle of Wisdom lived. When he arrived, he began to search for the eagle. Suddenly, he heard something flutter in the trees. It was the mighty Eagle of Wisdom. "Oh, Eagle of Wisdom, I seek to know your insight of the rainforest," said Hairan.

"What do you search for?" she asked.

"I want to know about the lions. Who are they? What happened?"he curiously asked.

"Years ago, the lions flourished here. The entire rainforest was occupied by them. But there was a chief pride, led by the last wild Barbary lion, who was called Bomani. Along with him was a lioness named Sitara and her sister who came from afar. He was the strongest and largest lion and was feared by all other lions.

But poachers came to the rainforest and killed many animals. Lots of creatures lost their lives. The national park was not able to protect every animal.

Then, one sad, dark night, Bomani was killed. It was too much for the park. The lions and rare animals were sent away to places called zoos, and the rainforest was abandoned by the humans," replied the wise eagle.

Hairan asked, "What about Sitara and her sister?"

"They were never seen again. Some say they might have been taken away, but I believe they ran away into the Unknown, the lands beyond the borders of the rainforest. But it is said that a lioness lives not too far away from the rainforest. Rumor has it that she's searching for a missing lion cub."

Hairan thanked the Eagle of Wisdom as he walked away. He had a hunch that he might be the missing lion cub and now had a quest to find his mother and ask why she had abandoned him. He ran quickly to the border of the rainforest, where there was a rusty, old metal fence with a large hole in the middle. Hairan quickly jumped through it to find himself in a wilderness. He tried to find the scent of something unusual.

After an hour of endless searching, Hairan finally found something. It had a strange scent. Eager to know what it was, he quickly followed it. The scent led to a large and eerie cave. But Hairan, who was unafraid, ran right in. As he went in deeper, he could hear a faint noise that grew louder and louder. Suddenly, in the shadows, there appeared two large ears and tusks. Its footsteps shook the cave. It was an elephant.

Hairan snarled as he let the elephant chase him. When the time was right, he pounced onto the elephant from the side. He held on tightly, biting its neck as hard as he could. The elephant tried to shake Hairan off by running with its full strength. Soon,

Hairan couldn't hold on any longer. He fell off and was lying on the ground. The elephant approached Hairan and was about to step on him. Then, suddenly, a mysterious creature pounced onto the elephant's back, finally taking it down. Hairan got up as he began to growl. The creature walked towards him and stared at him. Then Hairan knew what the creature was. It was a lioness."Are you my mother?"he asked excitedly. The lioness, who was Deepa, instantly recognized his pitch-black fur with its tints of grey, and his crystal blue eyes.

"No, I'm Deepa, the sister of your mother, Sitara. I've been searching for you. It's been 5 years!"she said excitedly.

"I can't believe it. I have an aunt!"he exclaimed. They ran to each other as they hugged. Deepa invited Hairan to her cave to talk. As they lay across from each other, Hairan asked, "If you're here, where is my mother?"

Deepa's happy smile soon became a sad frown. She turned her head away in sadness.

"What's wrong?" asked Hairan.

"She ran away into the Unknown. I wanted to follow her, but she was angry and roared at me. I was hurt, so I went back," she sadly said.

"But why would she do that to you? Why did she even abandon me?"he asked.

"It happened the day Bomani died. But I'm not sure why she acted that way," said Deepa.

"Do you have any idea where she went?"asked Hairan.

"If anywhere, I believe she went to the Gir Forest," she replied.

"What is the Gir Forest?" Hairan asked.

"Me and Sitara were born there. It's the sanctuary of all lions, where no evil dares to step foot in. I was just a cub when I left there. But Sitara told me how to get there," said Deepa.

"I hope your directions are right," said Hairan, staring into the distance.

Deepa asked, "What do you mean?"

"I'm going to go to this Gir Forest to find my mother," said Hairan.

"You're going into the Unknown? But it's dangerous," said Deepa discouragingly.

"I have to find her. But I'll need you to guide me. Will you join me?"asked Hairan.

"I really do want to see her again. I'll come along," said Deepa.

"Tomorrow, we'll start our journey to the Unknown. For now, we rest," said Hairan. He and Deepa fell asleep that night dreaming of what tomorrow would hold.

Soon, the dawning sun peaked on the horizon. The rainforest and its creatures started to arise, including Hairan and Deepa. They had just hunted a gazelle before starting their journey. After eating, Deepa began to investigate the trees around her.

"What are you looking for?" Hairan asked.

"I'm looking for umbrella thorn trees. Sitara told me we have to follow them until we reach our next location," she replied.

Hairan said, "I see one not too far ahead of us."

They quickly ran to it as Deepa said, "Okay, this is the first step. Now, we have to search for more." They followed the trees, which led them to a desert. After hours of walking, Hairan started to question if Deepa really knew the way to the Gir Forest. If not, then where were they really going?

They walked ahead, trying to stare into the distance. Not too far away, lay Rhino Rock. As they walked farther, a brisk breeze started to blow. It became stronger and stronger. They were unaware they were about to go through a sandstorm. They struggled to walk. Most animals would have given up, but Deepa and Hairan were not one of them. It was because they had determination. With full strength, they walked through the storm.

As the storm passed, they lay on the hot sand, barely breathing. They needed water fast. Right in front of them, there appeared to be a puddle of water. They crawled towards it with their remaining strength. They instantly began to slurp up the water, and were surprised at the fact they had survived the sandstorm.

They now returned to their journey, more wary of their surroundings. A few minutes later, they reached Rhino Rock. Since it was near nightfall, Hairan and Deepa began to look for shelter. After a while, Hairan then found an old, abandoned hut. He called his aunt, and they began to investigate it. After finding there was no danger, they slept on the front porch peacefully.

Chapter 3

An Oasis Adventure

When dawn came, they set off to continue their journey. To find the Gir Forest, they would have to go through the Lush Oasis. But it wouldn't be easy. They couldn't find any footprints or even a scent. They had no clue where the oasis was, and they were starving. It seemed they had no chance. Deepa lay in the sand, feeling hopeless and with no motivation. But Hairan still wasn't ready to give up.

There had to be some clue or hint that would guide them. He looked in all directions but saw nothing but endless sand dunes. Then something caught his eye. A single palm tree stood on the horizon. He began to run towards it. As he got closer and closer, more figures appeared. Hairan realized there was wild grass in the distance. Deepa weakly walked up to him."What are you doing here? We need to get out of here. I'm afraid we won't be able to make it to the Gir Forest," said Deepa frustratingly.

"I've been thinking. If all plants need water, how come this tree and the grass are able to survive in this desert? They must be getting water from underneath the ground. If we could possibly follow where the plants grow, it might lead us to the Lush Oasis!"said Hairan excitedly. Deepa agreed with him as they began to follow the plants. As they went farther, the plants and grass appeared to be greener and greener. They were given even more hope when they started to spot animal footprints. After stopping to eat and drink, they felt stronger and were able to carry on. But then they noticed something that scared them. Tracks of vehicles spanned the entire path.

"But Sitara said the oasis was a peaceful place where man and animal rarely encounter each other!"said Deepa in shock.

"The humans are moving closer and closer into animal territory. Things aren't like how they used to be in the past," said Hairan.

"Will you still go forward?"she asked.

"I'm determined to find my mother," he replied. They continued to walk on, hoping they would be able to make it to the oasis. Later, the sounds of vehicles filled the air, disrupting the silence. Hairan and Deepa were now in front of a city, which once was a small village. They hid in the bushes trying to avoid the humans.

"What do we do now? The humans are everywhere. There's no possible way to get through without being seen," she worriedly asked.

"We'll wait till nightfall. Hopefully, it will be easier then," he replied. In the meantime, they observed the city and the humans to plan a safe and fast route. Time flew by swiftly for Hairan and Deepa. Now, with the darkness of night, they would be able to sneak through the city. They walked through its gates and went into an alley. Swiftly but carefully, they ran from alley to alley, always looking for danger ahead of them. It seemed to be quite easy. But it wouldn't be like that for long.

They soon entered the heart of the city, which was the busiest and largest part of it. Shops and shacks overcrowded the thin roads. The buildings were conjoined, leaving no place to hide. It was a challenge that Hairan and Deepa were willing to accept. They slowly walked in between the shacks, trying to avoid hitting or smashing anything. They luckily got through the market and now began to run through the streets. With nowhere to hide, their only choice was to run. After a while, they were close to the exit. But they had one last obstacle in their way. Right ahead of them lay a sleeping police dog.

Hairan led Deepa, walking as quietly as he could. But he was so focused on the dog that he forgot what was in front of him. He stepped on an empty bottle, which immediately woke up the dog. Then it started to aggressively bark, alerting the police and the people nearby.

A group of men came out armed with guns. Hairan and Deepa frantically rushed to the exit, barely escaping. As the men's voices faded away, they entered a field of wheat, which was just outside the city. They could hear the footsteps and angry shouting of the men. They ran farther and farther until they could no longer hear them. They rested beneath a tree in the middle of the field. "We need to get out of this field quickly! The men are getting closer!"shouted Deepa worriedly. They began to wonder if they would make it out alive.

Then Hairan had an idea. He told Deepa to climb the tree so that she could see a way out of the field. As she held tightly on to a large branch, she stared around her. In the distance, there appeared to be a canal with two ships at a port. Deepa and Hairan ran ahead to the canal. They took a quick drink and then tried to find a way over it. But it seemed they wouldn't have enough time. The police were now at the port, searching for the lions. Out of fear, they quickly ran into the second ship and hid behind some boxes.

After searching around the area, the police went onto the first ship. They searched every single corner, leaving no space untouched. As they headed towards the second ship, a group of men spotted the police. The police questioned the group asking about the lions. The group said that they were there the whole time, and they didn't see anything. The police ran off to continue their search. A few minutes later, Hairan and Deepa realized the police were gone. They began to walk towards the exit, glad they had escaped. But then the ship's doors closed. Hairan and Deepa tried to search for another way out, but the only exit was through the doors. As the ship started to move away, they began to worry how they would ever find the Gir Forest now.

Chapter 4

Strange Land

It was now morning. The ship was pulling into a new port. The horn blared, startling Hairan and Deepa. They started to hear talking outside. They hid inside two crates. The voices outside were people unloading the ship. Hairan and Deepa were unaware of where they were. Hairan noticed light coming in from a small crease. He looked through it to see they were in another city, which was even larger than the first. Suddenly, they heard a strange sound coming towards them. It was a truck. The people loaded the crates onto the truck by using a large, strange machine. The truck began to drive away. "Where are we going? I can't see anything. I think we're lost," Deepa whispered.

"The humans loaded us onto one of their strange inventions. I wonder if we'll even make it out of here," said Hairan.

"All we can do is hope we will," said Deepa. Right after she said those words, the truck stopped. They began to worry what those doors would open to. Would they make it out alive and well? Everywhere was silent, and the only sound was their hearts rapidly thumping. Then the doors began to open. Hairan anxiously looked outside. To their surprise, they were in a storage barn for grain. There was no danger outside. The crates got unloaded and the truck drove away. Hairan and Deepa instantly got out. Right ahead of them were the giant doors. They tried to push against the doors, but they were securely locked.

The only other way to get out would be to go through one of the two large windows. There was one on each side of the building, but they were all the way on top. Hairan and Deepa tried to jump to get a grip, but it was no use. Hairan lay down on the ground, tired of leaping. He looked around the barn. Then he saw a stack of crates by one of the windows, which were long enough for them to leap from and reach the window. At that moment, he had a plan. He began to gather all the single crates and push them over to the stack."What are you doing?" Deepa asked sarcastically.

"I'm getting out of here. I need you to help me push these crates on top of each other," said Hairan. Deepa nodded but thought his plan wouldn't work. After they stacked the crates and made a stairway, Hairan led Deepa and they leaped through the window. It seemed his plan really did work. They tumbled into an abandoned alley. As they walked farther, the alley seemed to never end, until they reached an abandoned parking lot in the corner of the city. Hairan then had an idea. He and Deepa could climb up to the top of the parking lot and then see how to get out of the city. But Deepa was scared.

The parking lot was dark and eerie. Danger could be lurking at every corner. Hairan leaped into the parking lot, leaving Deepa alone outside. She took a deep breath and followed Hairan, holding him accountable if anything happened. As they entered the building, it got creepier as they went on. There were abandoned cars with broken windows. The lights along the walls flickered on and off. The floors had cracks inside. There was graffiti all over the walls. There was junk and trash in every corner. Deepa soon began to tremble. But Hairan didn't care.

After each experience, Hairan became more determined and brave. Soon, they reached the top. They overlooked the city to find an easy way out. This time, they looked for a route to avoid human contact, crowded paths, and areas with many obstacles. But they couldn't find any way out. Every foot of the city had some obstacle. It seemed impossible. While Deepa was distracted by the city's hustling, Hairan noticed something. There was a shallow trench nearby, which extended through the whole city to the desert outside. "Aunt Deepa," said Hairan, trying to get her to regain focus. "Do you see that trench in the corner there?"

"Yes, why do you ask?" replied Deepa.

"I think I have a plan. We can swim through the trench, which would lead us out of the city. It would get us out of here quickly, and it would also allow us to escape unseen. Do you agree with me?" asked Hairan. Deepa nodded as they commenced their plan. They jumped into the trench and swam swiftly out of the city. Hairan's plan had worked perfectly. Now out of the city, Hairan and Deepa were in a dry desert. They had no idea where they were. They decided to walk ahead to perhaps find a clue.

"Do you even have the slightest hint about where we are?"asked Hairan. Deepa shook her head as he continued. "Well, where was the next location after the oasis?"

"From the oasis, we were supposed to go through Colored Canyon, a canyon of many colors," she replied. After hours of walking tirelessly, they took a drink of water from a small stream. But the water wasn't thin and flowing. It seemed to have a grainy texture. Hairan sniffed the water and then took a closer look. He saw fine pieces of rocks of all shades of gold, orange, and brown. Hairan then assumed that the stream ran through the canyon. He decided to follow it to see if it led to the canyon. He was obviously right. They followed the stream and had reached the canyon. "Is this the place?"he asked.

Deepa replied excitedly, "Yes! This is the exact place!" They then proceeded into the canyon. At first, it appeared to be easy. There was one straight path. But then five paths appeared. They decided to go on the second path on the right. But that path led to more and more paths. They tried to get out but decided they would go around the canyon instead of going through it. Sadly, it was too late, and they were confused. They tried to climb the wall, but it was no use. The walls were too smooth. It seemed there would be no way out. After searching nonstop, it soon became night. Deepa gave up and Hairan went with her. His intelligence couldn't save him now. Suddenly, an unexpected opportunity came.

In the distance, Hairan saw what appeared to be fire. He and Deepa followed its light, which led them to rocks that resembled steps. He climbed up the rocks, with Deepa behind him. As he carefully peeked over the top, he saw humans sitting next to a fire. They wouldn't be able to pass if humans were there. Luckily, they had just thrown water on the fire and had gone to sleep in a tent.

After seeing it was clear, Hairan proceeded to the top as he slowly and quietly tried to pass the tent, with Deepa following in his footsteps. However, they were unaware that the humans could see their shadows through the tent. As they passed the tent, they heard rustling inside. They had been heard. Hairan and Deepa ran as fast as they could across the canyon top. Soon, they were out of sight but had reached a dead end.

They had to go to the other side of the canyon. There was no possible way across except for an old wooden bridge. The posts securing it were not properly put in and could fall out at any moment. Some of the bars seemed to have fallen out, and the remaining ones seemed to be unstable. It seemed they would have to make a hard choice. They would either have to try jumping across a long gorge or take a risk on the bridge. It was clear that the bridge was a safer option. But they had to hurry. The humans had decided to chase them, and they were almost near the bridge.

Hairan lifted his paw as he placed it on the first bar. He stepped forward slowly and carefully. The bridge began to shake. Hairan was scared but he had to continue. He walked cautiously, closely examining each step ahead. After seeing that Hairan was okay, Deepa followed his exact moves. They had soon reached the middle. The first half was quite easy, but the other side wasn't. There were only ten bars remaining, and it seemed they would have to leap to each one.

As Hairan began to think, Deepa shouted, "The humans! They're coming!" The voices of the men pierced the night's peaceful silence like a needle. Two shady figures were coming towards them with strange tubes that emitted light. Hairan had to think of a way fast. He quickly leaped, and he shouted, "Follow me!"He then leaped from bar to bar as each one broke off. Deepa quickly followed behind him, jumping on each bar before it fell too low.

The men ran onto the bridge, holding onto the ropes for support. One of them held out a strange, gray, flashing device while the other shone a light on Deepa, who was treading slowly behind them. Luckily, they were at the end of the bridge. It seemed they would make it. Hairan leaped as far as he could, reaching the other side. He suddenly heard Deepa crying for help. She was holding onto the edge with all her strength. Then Hairan noticed a tree by the edge. He pulled on one its branches and Deepa held on to it with her mouth. While holding on, she jumped onto the edge, letting go. Hairan and Deepa bit the ropes supporting the bridge. The bridge collapsed and the humans were no longer in sight. They ran breathlessly as far as they could.

After finally escaping, they began to look for a way out. As Deepa looked at the confusing gorge from above, Hairan spotted something right ahead. He tilted his head and looked at the weird shadows, trying to make out their shapes. He called Deepa over. They ran to the edge of a cliff and hid behind a bush. They realized it was a giant campground. They had found the very borders of the canyon. But it seemed they would not be able to escape.

After observing the camp, a thought came to Hairan. He and Deepa would be able to escape if they walked down on some boulders beside the cliff. They tried to come off the canyon without alerting the humans. But it was impossible. Not even Hairan could solve their situation. They lay down by the edge and watched the humans. Suddenly, they heard a loud noise. A man driving a jeep had come to see one of the campers. "Did you see any lions here? Two campers reported seeing a lion and lioness as in the photo here," said the man roughly. The camper shook his head as he said, "Sorry, sir. I haven't seen any lions, but I'll hang these around camp and let you know if something comes up."

"You don't mind if I look around, do you?"he asked.

"No, sir," the camper answered.

Hairan gasped as he said, "I think that human is looking for us, Deepa." But Deepa remained silent. He turned to see her frozen. She stared at the man, heavily panting. Her fur was raised up. "Is something wrong?" Hairan asked.

"He's here. We have to get out now!"said Deepa.

"The human? He can't see us all the way up here," said Hairan carelessly.

"That's no ordinary human," she mumbled. A tear escaped her eye as she continued. "He's a lion murderer."

"You know this guy? What happened?"he asked in shock.

Chapter 5

Sad Past

Deepa looked angry as she said in a quavering tone, "I was just four months old. The forest had caught on fire. My father had gone to find a way out. Sitara and I were told to stay in the cave with our mother. Moments later, we then started to hear roars and grunts. Our father was in trouble. While our mother looked for somewhere to hide us, Sitara and I ran through the forest. We then saw our father trying to wrestle the Dark Hunter, a man who was obsessed with tracking rare and dangerous animals. We watched our father fight the man.

We thought our father would win. But we were unaware of the weapons the man possessed.

The Dark Hunter pulled out a strange object. He smiled evilly. His green eyes shone in the shadows. He aimed the object at my father as it shot black balls at him. My father fell down instantly. We stared at his bloody body. Tears fell out of Sitara's eyes as I asked, "Dad's sleeping, right?"She ignored me as she continued to stare. She then stepped back. A snap echoed through the forest. Sitara had stepped on a twig. The Dark Hunter looked toward us. We had been spotted. We ran as fast as we could, trying to lose the Dark Hunter in the forest. Then our mother appeared. She hugged us while trying to keep her tears from falling, and she said, "Run north to the village. The humans there will keep you safe. I love you, my cubs."I asked if she was coming with us, and she replied, "I'll come to the village by sundown." Even though she reassured us, I felt she knew she was never going to see us again.

Then the shadow of the Dark Hunter appeared in the fire. We ran north for a good while until reaching the road. Right across laid the village's entrance. We went straight in. The villagers gave us water and a few scraps of meat as they put us in a shack. Sitara didn't touch a single piece of food. Instead, she went into the corner, weeping. Soon, the sunset. I waited and waited, but our mother did not come. I turned to Sitara as I asked, "When are Mom and Dad coming home?"

Sitara had remained silent as she tightened herself even more. I then jumped on her and asked, "When are they coming?"She pushed me off.

"They're never coming home. I didn't even get to say goodbye. I didn't get to tell them how much I love them," she had whispered to herself.

"They are going to come home," I said to her. Sitara had angrily shouted at me then. "They're dead! Killed by the Dark Hunter! Now, just leave me alone!"

"I then realized it was true. They really were never coming back. I lost happiness and joy that day. After that, we were captured by some people and taken far away. There, Sitara met your father and had you. It seemed things would once again be happy for me. But then the Dark Hunter and his men came and killed Bomani. I lost my sister Sitara, along with you. I thought he had been arrested, but it seems I was wrong. Now, he's after us, and it's unlikely we'll live if we don't leave."

Hairan looked around in haste. He remembered seeing a group of boulders near the edge of the camp. Even though it was very steep, it was the safest and most silent way to escape. Slowly and carefully, Hairan led Deepa to the ground. It seemed they would make it. They were just a few meters away from the ground. Then the giant rocks started to shift. The boulders were being supported on smaller rocks. Hairan had made a wrong step. He and Deepa tried to rush to the surface but failed. The boulders began to move even more and came crashing down. The sound was so loud that the whole canyon shook. It was obvious they had been heard.

The Dark Hunter ran through the camp at full speed. He reached the pile of boulders. He aimed his gun at it as he walked around it. This time, it seemed the lions really would be captured. But then the Dark Hunter had noticed something. There was a giant hole in the pile! Hairan and Deepa had escaped. He threw his hat on the ground as he shouted in rage. Meanwhile, Hairan and Deepa were having a way happier time. They were able to make it past the camp and were near the end of the canyon. They finally were able to get out of the canyon. Hairan and Deepa, who were tired from all that running, decided to stop for a drink at a small stream. As Hairan was drinking, he noticed Deepa looked very worried. "Are you worried he's going to catch us?"asked Hairan.

"We nearly got caught twice tonight. I don't think we'll be able to make it to the Gir Forest with the Dark Hunter following us. What if this is all just a big mistake? What if Sitara's not there? Even if she is, will she even care about us?"said Deepa hope-lessly.

"Don't talk like that. We must have hope. So, why must we worry about this Dark Hunter? My mother could be out there waiting for us. Don't give up," he said encouragingly. A small smile appeared on Deepa's face as she said, "I suppose you're right. Now, let's find a good shelter where we can hide." They ran off to look around.

Hairan spotted a farm in the distance. He called Deepa and they went to investigate. There was a large field of corn as far as the eye could see. It was the perfect place to hide. They ran inside quickly and searched for a bare area. Near the middle of the field, there was a large, dry area. However, Deepa was uncertain if the farm would really be a good hiding place. After walking around for a while, Hairan asked, "Isn't this a good place to hide?"

"I think this is a great place. But it's not good enough," replied Deepa.

"Why?" Hairan asked.

"I know the Dark Hunter. He has tracked and killed every single animal he desired. No matter where they hide, they always get caught. That is why we need a place better than this. It would be a little obvious to him if we hid in a field," she said. As Deepa turned to leave, the ground creaked when she stepped on it.

"What was that sound?" Hairan curiously asked.

"I think I stepped here, and it made a weird sound," she replied. Deepa once again placed her paw on the spot, and it creaked.

"It sounds hollow. I think there's something underneath there," he commented. Hairan ran to the spot and dug away the dirt, revealing a hidden trap door.

"What is it?"asked Deepa curiously.

"I don't know, but I think this metal thing might open it," said Hairan. He pulled the handle up with his mouth and it opened up. All they could see was darkness. Hairan leaned over to try to see what was inside. But he leaned in too much, causing him to tumble inside. Deepa called for him worriedly.

"I'm alive!"he shouted.

"How are you going to get out?"she asked.

Hairan quickly realized he was in an underground tunnel. He ran through it to see where it would lead. He discovered a staircase at the end, and there was a trap door. He opened it and saw he was at the edge of the field, with a stream nearby. He exited and ran back to Deepa, who was looking down into the tunnel. She jumped as if she had seen a ghost when she saw Hairan in front of her. Hairan then explained to her what happened. They then decided to hide in there.

Hairan led Deepa to the other end of the tunnel and they walked down the staircase. The trap door closed shut as they were left in complete darkness. "It's so dark in here. We should go back to the surface," said Deepa trembling.

"Let's explore for a little while to see if we could stay here for the night. This is a great place to hide. The Dark Hunter would never suspect we're here," Hairan said. Then Hairan noticed a flashing light ahead in a hidden part of the tunnel. He ran towards it and stood in awe. The flashing light came from above and reflected on the walls of the tunnel, which were adorned with precious metals that glittered like a sea of glass. As they stood frozen in awe of the beauty, they heard a distant noise. It was the Dark Hunter. They quickly ran into the corner and hid. The noise stopped as fast thuds headed towards them. Soon, the thuds were right above them. The Dark Hunter had reached the dry area.

"Will we make it?" That was the only question running through the poor lions' heads. Everything seemed to go silent. The only sound was their heavy breathing. They tried to push themselves even deeper into the corner, but they couldn't.

"Where are you? Come out, little lions!"shouted the Dark Hunter. After seeing they weren't there, the evil man ran off to continue searching.

Hairan and Deepa were overjoyed that the Dark Hunter did not discover their hiding place. They sighed in relief as Deepa said, "You were right. I can't believe we made it. Maybe we do have a chance."They then slept peacefully, knowing they had a chance to get out of there. But things would become harder for them. They were reported in the local news, which soon went worldwide. Poachers and hunters would be after Deepa and especially Hairan. Nevertheless, they would continue for they had hope like no other. Nothing would get in their way. Not even the dangers they would face in the morning. At dawn, they set off on their journey. As they walked out of the cornfield, Hairan asked, "Where do we go next?"

"We must go through the Timna Valley. In order to find it, we have to look for cypress trees. They are native to the valley, but I'm sure there might be some out here," she said.

"What do cypress trees look like?" Hairan asked.

Deepa said, "I don't really remember. But I recall Sitara saying they had a grayish-brown bark and a really strong, sweet smell."

Hairan looked around but could only see a dry, barren desert. There was not a single tree in sight. Then the wind blew towards him. He picked up a slight scent he had never smelled before. Its scent was like the strong and fresh smell of burning wood in a forest, with accents of sandalwood. He lifted his head as he looked in the direction the breeze was coming from. He ran ahead, telling Deepa to follow him.

After running for a while, they noticed a tree. The scent that Hairan had smelled became stronger. He had found a cypress tree! As he looked into the distance, he noticed a small group of trees. Another cypress was there. They followed the trail, which led them to a steep, rocky mountain wall. On it, there were large pieces of rocks, which made an uneven stairway. If they walked correctly, Hairan and Deepa would be able to get safely up. But after their previous experience with climbing, they knew they had to be extremely careful. This time, Deepa led Hairan, slowly stepping on each rock. It seemed everything would go well.

They were just a short distance away from the top. However, the next two rocks ahead were too small for them, and they wouldn't be able to jump across because the gap between them was wide. They began to worry. They were high up on the mountain cliff. It was too risky to go back down. Even though they were stuck and could possibly die, they had learned that in every situation, there is always a way out.

Hairan looked around and felt something scratch against his head. Above him was a huge old tree growing from between the rocks. He then had an idea. If he held on to a branch, he could climb up the tree and reach the top of the mountain! He then told Deepa his plan. Hairan held onto it and Deepa jumped onto the branch and reached the top. Then Hairan quickly climbed up, finally reaching the top. They stood at the very top and overlooked the valley. Clusters of cypress trees spotted the sand-filled valley. Desert shrubs and plants grew beside the small lakes within the area. After admiring the beauty of the valley, they walked for a while. They saw the exit not too far away. However, they were unaware that tourists would be there.

Hairan and Deepa ran ahead, unaware of the danger lurking. Suddenly, they were noticed by a group of tourists. The humans ran back and forth screaming. Frightened by their screaming, Hairan and Deepa ran as fast as they could, and they looked for a place to hide. They ran behind a rock. "This place is full of humans. We can't run mindlessly. We have to pay attention to our surroundings and its inhabitants," Deepa advised.

After the humans were out of sight, the lions continued to head towards the exit; only this time, they were very alert. After a while, they finally reached the giant rock, which was in the center of the park. Even though it was evening, Hairan and Deepa wanted to leave the valley as soon as possible. They planned to walk all night. But it seemed things would not go their way.

A noise echoed through the valley. It was the very same noise they had heard yesterday. The Dark Hunter had come. They had to hide quickly. Luckily, the valley was home to many ancient copper mines, which were like mazes. The mines would make the perfect hiding place. Hairan spotted a tunnel not too far away. They quickly ran inside and looked for somewhere to hide. There were two routes ahead of them. Hairan went to the right while Deepa went to the left. But the tunnels led to even more tunnels. The mine was more complex than they thought it would be.

They both decided to choose two separate paths so that one of them could be saved without getting caught. Not too long after, they began to hear a voice and footsteps in the tunnels. The Dark Hunter was in the mine. He walked through the tunnel Hairan had gone through. He went into each route searching for the lions. He searched all the routes of Hairan's side of the tunnel. Only one tunnel was left, and it happened to be the one Hairan was hiding in. The Dark Hunter jumped out and pointed his gun. But nothing was there except for a cart. It seemed the only place Hairan could be hiding was beneath it.

The Dark Hunter kicked the cart as he aimed his gun at it. But nothing was under it. He then began to walk farther down the tunnel. At the end of the tunnel, there was a small pit, which Hairan was hiding in. As the Dark Hunter was about to reach the end of the tunnel, a roar echoed through the cave. Deepa had escaped while the Dark Hunter was searching for them in the tunnel, and she was calling Hairan.

The Dark Hunter then ran out after hearing her roar. She heard the Dark Hunter coming and she ran away, searching for somewhere to hide. She stumbled upon a hidden lake. She quickly jumped into the water, trying to hold her breath as long as she could. The Dark Hunter stood above the lake as he tried to look into the water. Soon, Deepa struggled to hold her breath. Luckily, the Dark Hunter ran off to continue searching. After seeing that he had left, Deepa went to the surface, gasping for air. She then went to look for Hairan. She followed his scent, which led her to a cave. Inside was Hairan.

"I thought you were caught. How did you make it?"asked Deepa, feeling relieved. Hairan told her how he had escaped while the Dark Hunter was after her. They then went to sleep, hoping the next day wouldn't be so hard. When morning came, Hairan and Deepa woke up to continue their journey. After seeing nobody in sight, they went outside. They ran from rock to rock to avoid being seen. They soon safely made it out. As they rested beneath an olive tree, Hairan asked, "Where is our next location?"

"We have to go through the old, abandoned city of Petra. We have to look for the tracks of the strange objects that humans ride in," she replied. They looked around. Hairan then noticed a group of jeep tracks that were all heading east. They ran as fast as they could before the tracks could get covered with sand. After a while, however, the tracks did get covered by the desert sand. Hairan and Deepa were lost in the middle of a desert. Tired and thirsty, they searched for water. They found a small oasis surrounded by dale trees. They quickly ran to it and slurped up water. After drinking, Hairan noticed something in the distance. The jeeps were driving towards this giant pink rock formation. Hairan and Deepa carefully followed them. They realized the pink rock was the city of Petra. As the group of jeeps drove on, they quickly snuck through, knowing it wouldn't be easy to get through Petra. They saw a group of tourists ahead. Hairan and Deepa quickly ran inside one of the old, abandoned houses.

When they were inside, Deepa inadvertently pushed a small clay pot and it fell to the ground. Its clatter destroyed the silence. They had nowhere to hide. The shadow of a human appeared on the wall. Voices quietly murmured as slow footsteps headed towards them. A man abruptly appeared inside the house unexpectedly, holding a stick. He called out and looked around, but no one was there. Luckily, they escaped through a window and ran away just in time. They hid behind a boulder, panting, as Hairan said, "We have to get out of here now. There are too many humans here. It will be impossible to leave without being seen."

"You're right. But we're too deep in it. We have to get out," said Deepa.

"We should wait until night. It might be safer then," Hairan advised. Deepa nodded her head in agreement, and when evening came, they ran to the grasslands. Tall grass and bushes were everywhere. They saw an old wooden sign ahead, beside a road. "What is that ahead?"asked Hairan. They went to examine it.

"Oh my! I recognize this sign. It will lead us to the Mountain of Junipers, one of most luscious places on Earth," replied Deepa. They ran forward as they watched the horizon. Nothing green lay in the distance. Only sand was in sight.

"Are you sure this is the right way? There appears to be no 'Mountain of Junipers,'" Hairan said doubtfully.

"I'm sure this is the right way!" Deepa reassured him.

They then proceeded to walk down the road. After walking for hours, morning soon came. The sun scorched the path, causing cracks to appear in it. The sunlight was so bright it could blind someone if they looked up for too long. Deepa and Hairan could barely walk from the heat and dehydration. They needed water quickly. They would not make it if they didn't get water soon. But no water was in sight. Deepa soon fell down, motionless and barely breathing. "So thirsty; need water," she mumbled, heavily panting.

"We can't give up yet, even though we might die of thirst," Hairan said. But he could not continue either. He also stumbled and fell. He crawled with his remaining strength, but his eyes started to grow dim. The sounds around him slowly started to disappear. He and Deepa fainted. They would need to find water quickly if they wanted to survive.

Suddenly, they were awakened by loud thunder, and rain was falling on their fur. They quickly slurped up some water. Drenching wet, they staggered in the rain, looking for shelter. After walking for a while, the rain finally stopped. They looked ahead to see a mountain covered in green in front of them. It was the most luscious place they had seen. Bird calls and noises echoed through the mountain. It was unbelievable that such a place could be in the middle of a desert. "I think we're at the foothills of the Mountain of Junipers," said Hairan, frozen by the sight of it.

They quickly ran up the mountain. As they walked among the trees, it was even more beautiful. Tall junipers reaching to the sky covered the mountain. The leaves of the trees were so thick that not even a single beam of light could penetrate the canopy. The grasses were adorned with a wide variety of colored flowers. The mountain was just one of the wonders of the Unknown. They would see many more, each more beautiful than the first. After looking for a while, they found a cave not too far away, and they quickly fell asleep exhausted. But they wouldn't be asleep for long.

Chapter 6

A Secret Uncovered

Early in the morning, Deepa harshly nudged Hairan as she whispered in his ear, "Wake up! There are humans outside!" He instantly woke up after hearing those words. The two lions glanced outside to see people.

"I have an idea. Just follow me," said Hairan. He pushed down a rock to distract them. The sound alerted the humans.

"Are you crazy? They just heard us!" said Deepa fearfully. Suddenly, footsteps, along with voices, headed towards them. They quickly ran through the back exit of the cave. Deepa, having no other choice, followed him. Hairan ran as fast as he could and Deepa followed behind him. After running for a while, they rested beneath some trees.

"Every single day, we face some kind of danger. What if we don't get out of it next time? I'm tired of this. I wish I was back home," said Deepa angrily.

"Forget what happened. Let's continue the journey," replied Hairan.

They ran far from the mountain until it was out of sight. Hairan asked, "Where do we go next?" But Deepa remained silent as she stared at the ground. "Hello? Is something wrong?" asked Hairan. Deepa then shook her head and noticed a stream nearby. She said, "This stream will lead us to some caves we have to go through." Hairan realized she was troubled.

"What's wrong? You can tell me. We're family," said Hairan.

Deepa murmured, "Nothing. I'm fine."

Hairan then said, "Aunt Deepa! Tell me please. You can trust me."

Deepa said, "What if I told you Sitara isn't alive?"

Hairan froze as he said, "What do you mean? Everything is fine. Right?"

Tears began to fall from her eyes as she said, "Nothing is fine! The truth is this: Two days after Sitara ran off, I was determined to see her. Even though she had hurt me, I had to go to her. She was more than a sister. She was like a mother to me. When my parents died, she raised me. Our bond was close. How could I leave her? I ran into the wilderness searching for her. I followed her scent and eventually found her. But I was too late.

"In a cage, I saw her lying down. I pushed through the bars of the cage and nudged her motionless body as I whispered, 'Wake up.' But there was no answer and not a single movement. That's when I saw the humans talking. In their hands was the black, loud object that kills animals. At that moment, my mind was spinning. I knew she was no more. The only reason I came on this journey was because of you, and I didn't have the courage to tell you that your mother was dead! I didn't want you to go into the wilderness. You're all I have of her. Ever since I met you, I vowed to myself to always protect and stay by your side no matter what. But now we are being attacked from every corner. The Dark Hunter and people have been on our tails, and each day it becomes more dangerous. I've kept the truth to myself to give you some hope. But I can't go on like this anymore! I'm sorry we can't find your mother."

Tears poured from her red eyes like a waterfall. Her face was drenched in tears. Hairan remained frozen. He didn't make a single movement. Thoughts rushed through his head. He had never felt so confused since Musafa told him about his past. "This whole journey was purposeless. So many risks for nothing! I should've stayed home with my pack!"he thought to himself.

Then he turned to Deepa who was crying heavily. He looked at her for a second as he pushed all his thoughts away. He then ran and hugged her. "Don't cry. This is my fault and I brought you here. I shouldn't have come here!"said Hairan.

"It's not your fault. It's mine! If I had told you the truth, we would not be here," said Deepa tearfully.

"Well, we have already done what we have done. All we can do now is affect the future," said Hairan.

"Well, what should we do now?"asked Deepa worriedly.

"We've gone too far and have no other choice but to go ahead. It would be too far and dangerous to go back home. The Gir Forest is a place where we can have freedom, as you said. If we go there, we will have freedom from the hunters," said Hairan, sighing.

As they walked ahead, Hairan began to behave strangely. Instead of being talkative, he remained silent. Deepa realized Hairan was sad, just like she was. "Don't be so sad, Hairan. We have each other at least. Right?" said Deepa, trying to comfort him. Hairan still remained silent with his head down low. But he didn't hear Deepa's words. His thoughts filled his mind so much, the entire world seemed to be mute. Suddenly, his thoughts were interrupted.

"Look! The caves are right ahead!" said Deepa.

"Okay. Let's continue searching," said Hairan sadly. After following the stream, they were led to the giant dark caves. There were so many openings, but the biggest one was in the middle. They quickly went through it. Inside, the cave was pitch black. You couldn't see anything. The ground was damp. It was very scary. After walking in the dark for a while, they noticed that a part of the cave was brightly lit up. They curiously and quietly went towards it. Suddenly, weird whirring sounds echoed through the cave. Shadows were right ahead of them, accompanied by human voices. They were heading towards them.

"Hairan! There are humans here. We have to get through the cave quickly," Deepa said worriedly. She ran out at full speed. She exited the cave on the other side and stopped a good distance away from it. She then turned to see if Hairan was behind her. But he was nowhere in sight! He was in the cave with the humans! She ran with all her might back to the cave. She heard Hairan growling when she entered it. Her heart raced and thumped fast. She was nearly about to faint. She saw the shadows of Hairan and the humans. Deepa glanced at Hairan who was cornered by them. Before she could even reach him, a man hit Hairan with a huge object that was in the cave. The lion let out a roar as he fell down. Deepa instantly froze, forgetting about her surroundings. It was Sitara all over again. But she couldn't bear it. She then looked at the humans tearfully and motionless. They knocked her out with a quick blow to the head.

A beam of light shone onto Deepa's face. She suddenly opened her eyes to find herself in the back of a truck. She was somehow alive. As she got up, right next to her was Hairan, staring through the window at the night sky. "I'm sorry," said Hairan sadly.

"What do you mean?"asked Deepa.

"You know what I mean. This is all my fault. If only I was paying attention, we wouldn't have gotten caught by the humans. Now, we're in this thing and are most likely headed to some dangerous place," replied Hairan.

"I know you're sad about the truth. Please tell me what's wrong. I might be able to help you," said Deepa.

"I think this has all been a mistake. I miss my pack. Sure, Zahara and Jabari weren't my real parents. But they felt like a true mother and father. I didn't even get to say goodbye to them. I just ran off, angry for no reason. Then, if we hadn't come out here, the Dark Hunter would never know about us and wouldn't be chasing us. Because of my stupid decision, we are both in danger and are headed to some dangerous human place!"said Hairan regretfully.

"You miss your pack and regret coming here? Is that why you were so distracted?"asked Deepa. Hairan glanced at her and he slightly nodded. "It's not really your fault. It's my fault. I had the directions and I led you here. So, it's both of our faults really," added Deepa.

Hairan continued to silently stare outside. As Deepa tried to get up, she couldn't. She was tied up with thick rope. She gnawed at the rope until she was free. Hairan did the same. They pushed against the door, which wasn't properly locked. The doors then flew open, and they jumped out. The driver and his companion stopped and came out to see what had happened. They saw the lions running into a pasture nearby. They furiously shot bullets at the lions.

Hairan and Deepa ran as fast as they could and luckily were not hit. As they wandered through the field, they could see nothing but endless, dry, brown grass reaching to the light blue sky. Suddenly, they heard something fly through the air. It was a bullet! The bullet hit Deepa, grazing and injuring her leg. She moaned loudly as she fell to the ground. Then they heard the voices of the men approaching them. The humans had not given up. There was no time; Hairan and Deepa needed somewhere to hide, and quickly. "I can't walk. I cannot bear the pain. Go on without me before they get you!"shouted Deepa.

"You are going to get out of here!" replied Hairan. He placed Deepa's paws on his back, supporting her so that they could go as fast as they could. They ran in the opposite direction of where the noise was coming from. Hairan watched from the tall grass and saw the humans walking through the field. He then gently placed Deepa onto the ground. While Deepa rested, Hairan began to wonder what they would do. How would they avoid humans? What if they were caught again? Would they even make it to the Gir Forest? He was thinking so much that he forgot about the time. It was night and he still didn't know what to do. As he laid his head down to sleep, he had a strange dream. He dreamt he was back home in the grasslands. However, the sky was dark gray, and the sun wasn't visible. Hairan then heard Deepa calling out for him. He followed her voice to see her surrounded by humans. Hairan wanted to save her, but fear overcame him. He watched as they dragged her off and put her into their strange object and then drove away. He instantly woke up, panting heavily.

"What's wrong?" asked Deepa, half awake.

"Nothing," replied Hairan, still shocked by his dream. As he looked at the dawn sky, he decided to go hunting. Perhaps it would take his mind off the dream. As he searched for animals, he spotted a markhor buck that had wandered from his herd. He grazed on the grass without a care, knowing it was risky. As Hairan stared at him, he felt the markhor was just like how he was before—careless and taking risks, thinking he'd always get out of his problems. Well, the reckless goat had to be taught a lesson. Hairan pounced on the markhor and bit his neck before he could do anything. He then fell to the ground as Hairan dragged him to the field. He placed the markhor before Deepa, saying, "I found some goat that wandered off from his herd. I decided to hunt him for breakfast."

However, Deepa stared at the markhor in shock. "What's wrong?" asked Hairan, confused by Deepa's reaction.

"This is one of the long, curly horned goats Sitara told me about! We might be closer to the Gir Forest than I thought! We should reach there in a short while if I'm correct! But it might take a little longer with this leg of mine," added Deepa as she tried to stand.

After they ate their fill, Hairan helped Deepa walk outside to continue their journey. "Well, where do we go next?" asked Hairan.

"We have to go through the Golden Delta. We're close to it," answered Deepa.

"The Golden Delta?" asked Hairan curiously.

"There's supposed be a large river that goes across this entire region. If we follow it, it's supposed to lead us to the delta," she replied.

"I heard water rushing by the edge of the field. It sounded like a river to me," Hairan said.

They went to the edge of the field as fast as they could. They then saw the river, which stretched out to the horizon. They were in shock. It had taken so long to cross the field, but that was nothing compared to the distance ahead. As night approached, they were still by the shore, and they didn't even get far. They noticed a shady tree along the way. "We'll rest here and continue at sunrise," said Hairan, determined to reach the Golden Delta as soon as possible. When the sun peaked on the horizon, Hairan got up and drank some water. Suddenly, he began to hear various strange sounds. Startled by the noise, he went to investigate.

The sound came from cows that were grazing in a pasture. A fence, spanning for miles, separated him from them. Hairan noticed something weird. He saw a shed full of carts, with ropes to pull them. Suddenly, he got an idea. He could use the cart to pull Deepa with his strong jaws. It would be easier, safer, and faster than helping her walk. But it would be risky as well. Hairan spotted a group of humans sleeping beneath a tree at the end of the enclosed area. If the cows saw him, they would alert the humans. Staring at the farm, he said to himself, "Never again." As he turned to leave, he glanced back at the carts. If he was really careful, perhaps he could get out safe and sound.

Suddenly, he heard a voice say, "What are you doing?"

He turned around to see Deepa weakly bracing herself against a tree. "I'm going to get that pulling thing. It will make the journey safer and faster," said Hairan. They went through the front gate

44

stealthily. Hairan helped Deepa get into the cart and he pulled the rope. It was faster and easier than he expected. Hairan quickly but quietly pulled the cart outside as they continued the journey. After a few hours of walking, they were near the Golden Delta. Small pieces of shiny objects glimmered in the sun.

"We're getting close to the delta. Those shiny objects are gold," said Deepa. But one obstacle blocked them from the delta. The area ahead was a marshland. The sticky mud and thick bushy plants would make it hard to pass through with the cart. "What do we do now?" asked Deepa.

"The entire area ahead is a marshland. We have no other choice but to go ahead," replied Hairan.

"Wait," said Deepa, closely investigating the area. "Look, some parts of this marshland are dry. If we move correctly, we can avoid the wet areas," she added. Hairan slowly pulled the cart ahead until he reached the start of the marsh. Right ahead was a dry piece of land. But murky, thick water separated them from the patch.

"We can't get over this! The distance between is too long. The pulling thing will obviously get stuck," said Hairan, backing away.

"We can run over it fast. Try it," said Deepa encouragingly.

"No, I can't do this. This is just too risky," replied Hairan.

"Then I'll do it," said Deepa, pushing against the cart to get Hairan to move ahead.

"What are you doing?" replied Hairan worriedly.

"I'm getting us to the delta!" answered Deepa. After Deepa pushed with all her strength, Hairan's paws finally touched the marsh. Startled, he quickly ran over the water onto the dry patch. "See, if you run quickly to each patch, you'll get there safely," said Deepa.

"Fine, I'll do it," answered Hairan. He went from patch to patch until he finally reached the shore. As he walked onto the shore, still tugging the cart, they realized they had finally reached the Golden Delta. It was more beautiful than they had ever expected. Specks of gold spotted the entire delta, which caused it to glisten more than the sun. If they looked directly into it, they would be blinded. Various types of wildflowers dotted the delta, decorating it. Storks filled the area, along with markhors. Tall green trees with welcoming boughs lined the landscape. Deepa was truly in awe, but Hairan didn't care for the beauty around them. They walked through the long delta until night. They were nearly at the end, and they planned to stop soon.

"Do you see anywhere to stop?" Hairan asked.

"I wasn't really paying attention. I was looking at those flowers over there," replied Deepa. Hairan groaned as he continued to look around. "Wait, I see something over there!" said Deepa, looking at her side. An old wooden hut was right in front of them. Nearly half of it was broken, but the roof would provide enough shelter. It was covered in moss. Thick flowers and bushes surrounded it, making it hidden. Hairan pulled the cart inside it as he helped Deepa out. After a few minutes, Deepa fell fast asleep. But Hairan was wide awake. He stared at the delta. It was even more beautiful and bright in the night. But he had no joy or excitement for it. As he stared at the night sky, memories of his old pack flickered in his mind. He slightly chuckled as he remembered the day Zahara taught him to hunt. He was chasing after a rabbit but accidentally bumped into a tree. A beehive fell on him and he went mad. Then he remembered Zahara helping him take it off. It was all worth it for the honey though.

The moment quickly passed as he pouted. He felt guilty for leaving his pack to go on a wild chase for nothing. They truly loved and cared for him. Zahara and Jabari were ready every moment of every day to give their lives for Hairan. They had demonstrated it various times. But what did he do for them? He abandoned the ones who loved and cared for him. The thought just made him start to cry. As tears started to fall from his eyes, he laid his head down. At dawn, they were awakened by the sound of storks flapping their wings. They decided to leave early to go looking for the Great Mountains, a sign they were approaching the Gir Forest. Hairan pulled the cart, following a trail hoping it would lead to the Great Mountains.

After walking for hours nonstop, they finally saw the mountains ahead. They could already feel the cool mountain breeze. Tired and weary, Hairan wanted to run up the mountains quickly, but he had to pull Deepa because she was still weak. He began to look for a faster route to get up. Then he spotted something. There was a group of boulders that led to a pathway to climb up the mountains. So, they decided to head towards the boulders. However, the boulders were extremely rough, and it would be hard for the cart to go over. Would Hairan be willing to take the risk? He gazed at the boulders fearfully. Hairan lifted his paw and took a step forward. He then began to run towards the mountains.

As he reached the first boulder, he took a deep breath and slowly walked up. The bottom wasn't hard, but as it went up, it became more uneven. Hairan had to pull the cart up with his jaws while doing all this. He placed his paw on a flat rock as he pulled the cart slowly and carefully. He then took one more step forward and then another.

As he got near to the middle, he heard rocks crumbling below him. One of the cart's wheels was stuck! A huge, pointy rock blocked the way. Deepa began to worry while Hairan slowly tried to pull the cart up, but it seemed he couldn't get out of the situation. Suddenly, the wheel fell off as Hairan ran up as fast as he could to the top. He made it to the pathway and he and Deepa watched the wheel tumble down. They then turned to the cart as Deepa asked, "What are we going to do? Will the pulling thing still work?"

"I think so," said Hairan, walking slowly to see what would happen. "It seems we'll just be a little slower now. But other than that, it will work fine," said Hairan reassuringly. He dragged the cart and he slowly walked up towards the pathway. That was when he realized that the pathway was not sturdy. It was long and thin with very little support.

Hairan froze in fear as he approached the pathway to the mountain. His heart was beating like a drum as he stared at the ground. He felt it was a mistake. He was sure he wouldn't make it if he fell down. He gulped as he slowly walked backwards.

"What are you doing?" asked Deepa, confused by his actions.

"Can't you see? We're so high from the ground, and this path is so thin. It won't be able to hold our weight, and if we fall, there's no way we'll survive that," said Hairan worriedly.

"We'll be fine. Remember when we crossed the old bridge back at Colored Canyon? It seemed we wouldn't make it, yet we did because we planned it out and were careful. This path is nothing compared to the one before," said Deepa encouragingly.

Hairan remained silent as he continued to back out. Then Deepa slowly got out of the cart since she was regaining her strength.

"What are you doing?" said Hairan angrily.

"I'm going over since you're so scared. I don't understand what happened to you! You used to be so outgoing, creative, and full of hope. You made risky plans no other lion would do, and you still believed you would make it through somehow! What happened to that Hairan? Now, I'm stuck with this Hairan with no care, no motivation. The old Hairan was different. I need that Hairan here; I'm sure he would get over this smoothly. In fact, he would get through all of this as if it were nothing!" argued Deepa.

"Well, that Hairan is dead. I was foolish to do all those stunts. I was foolish to leave my pack. I was foolish in every single act I've done ever since I went on this useless quest. I was filled with false hope. I was filled with lies!" roared Hairan, struggling to keep in his tears.

"Look, I'm sorry, Hairan. I didn't mean to say those things," said Deepa regretfully. "If this is anyone's fault, it's mine. I never should've lied to you. I should have told you the truth since we met," she added.

Then Hairan gripped onto the ground as he growled, staring ahead. He went up the pathway to the mountains without a care, with Deepa limping behind. When he reached the mountain top, Hairan breathed a sigh of relief. Then he walked on without saying a single word. Deepa was certain Hairan was hurt by the truth about Sitara, and he had an unquestionable reason why. He had left his pack, his only family, searching for his mother who wasn't even alive. For five years, he was with them. Then he left them without saying a word.

Deepa glanced back at Hairan as she placed herself in his position. She realized that she would be as hurt and sad as he was. As evening approached, they stopped in a small cave. Deepa watched Hairan as he fell asleep. She regretted what she had said on the path. It seemed it hurt him even more. All she could do was hope tomorrow would be better.

At dawn, they set off to get down the mountain. However, getting down wouldn't be as easy as they thought, since it was rocky and harsh. They could easily lose control and cause an avalanche if they made a single wrong move. They began to look for other safer ways to get down. They spent a long time searching for another route but found nothing. Deepa was afraid to ask Hairan what they should do. They hadn't talked all morning and she felt ashamed to even say one word to him because of what happened yesterday.

"Hairan, what should we do now? I can't find any way down," said Deepa nervously.

"We'll leap onto the smoother parts of the rocky mountain until we reach the bottom" said Hairan. He then leaped cautiously and slowly from place to place, always looking for the safest spot to land, with Deepa following behind him. After struggling for a while, they finally reached the bottom of the mountain where there was a road.

"I'm going to look for somewhere to rest," said Hairan angrily. He then ran off, leaving Deepa alone. Suddenly, a noise echoed throughout the area. Hairan raised his head as he turned around. He saw Deepa limping towards him.

"Run!" Deepa shouted. In the distance, they saw a truck not too far away. Hairan instantly ran to Deepa as he helped her to run faster. Sadly, they still weren't quick enough. The vehicle was gaining on them. Hairan ran with all his might and strength.

"What are we going to do? This thing is going to reach us!" said Deepa.

"Wait, I have a plan, but it's risky. However, it's the only choice we have," said Hairan. They detoured from the road and went into the jungle thickets. The bushes and rough ground would certainly stop those who were chasing them, or so they thought. The humans seemed to be willing to take any risk to reach the lions. They pompously went after them. Hairan and Deepa began to worry but still had a spark of hope in them.

Not too far ahead, there was a big fallen tree covered in

brushes. A large hole was underneath. The people wouldn't be able to go over it or suspect them there. But a low hanging branch had scraped Deepa's wound and it began to bleed again. They had temporarily lost the humans, but they had very little time until they were found again.

"What happened?" asked Hairan worriedly.

"The branch brushed against my injured leg. I can't go on. I want you to reach the Gir Forest safely. That is my last and final wish," said Deepa calmly. The truck had found them again. Fear struck Hairan's heart and took control of him. He was confused. He ran towards the tree until he stopped in his tracks. He got control of his instincts as he turned around.

"What have I done?" he asked himself as he ran back to Deepa. But she was gone. The humans had captured her. The truck wasn't too far away. "There is still a chance," he said in his mind, trying to comfort himself. But those words were lies, and he knew it. He chased after the truck with his remaining strength until he fainted.

Suddenly, he woke up as vultures began to land on him. He roared angrily as they flew away. He began to cry as he thought in his mind, "What have I done? I let fear and anger control me! If I didn't run away in anger, she would've been here! If I didn't run away in fear, she would've been here! She was right. I am useless and foolish. Now, I've made the most foolish decision of my life. It was just like in my dream. She did so much for me. She nearly died for me. She's like a mother. I've been searching for a mother, yet I always had one with me. Now, I have no one. No pack, no mother. Just me. This is it," he told himself.

He turned towards the thick jungle terrain as he went to it in tears. He could barely walk. It was as if he had no strength in him. He went down the trail as he glanced back. Now, all he could do was fulfill Deepa's final wish.

Chapter 7

Another Chance?

Hairan had just entered the jungle. As he stared at the horizon, he could barely see it. The foliage and trees were so thick that all he could see was a piece of the sun. He remembered, every dawn, he and Deepa would stare at the horizon. Every time they looked at it, it would give them hope. But it seemed all hope was lost. "What am I doing? I don't deserve this. I don't deserve to find the Gir Forest without her. This is pointless. I'll wander forever! I'll be a lone lion from now on. Even after how I treated her, she still wanted me to have a good life." He truly was angry at himself. He didn't even know where he was going. All he knew was that he wasn't going to the Gir Forest.

All day, he thought about Deepa. He remembered all the adventures they had and the things they encountered. Those were good, memorable times. If only he had been grateful enough for what he had. Soon, the sunny skies became dark. Thunder and gray filled the sky. Not a single beam of sunlight was visible. Hairan quickly ran into a small moss-covered cave. As he stared at the rain pouring outside, he huddled deeper into the cave. The rain poured until nightfall. The land was flooded and marshy. He slowly fell asleep, uncertain of the new day ahead.

A cold drop of water fell on Hairan's nose. He suddenly woke up and looked around. The waters had receded, and the land had dried up. It was time to continue his wandering. Then an unexpected event occurred. He was walking aimlessly through the jungle. He hadn't eaten for a while and was growing weak. He then fell down, unable to get up. His eyes grew dim. All around him faded. He suddenly woke up as he found himself in a cage. He was in complete darkness, but he could smell something. There was a bowl of meat across from him. He quickly ran to it and gobbled it up. He then walked around the cage wondering how he had gotten there. But all he knew was that he would escape. He pushed against the cage, but it was too sturdy. Then he realized its weakness. A simple latch door kept the cage closed. He used a bone from the meat and pushed it through the cage's bars. Hairan then flipped the latch, opening the cage.

When he looked outside, he was in shock. He saw dozens of cages around him. In front of him was a giant red and white tent covered in lights. He heard distant laughter coming from it. He carefully and stealthily crept into a corner unseen, and he looked in. When he entered it, he was in shock. Animals of all kinds were being forced to do dangerous stunts. Humans surrounded them, laughing and shouting. The poor creatures were clearly in pain, but the people ignored them.

A few minutes later, all the humans left except for a few. Then it became more horrendous. The people started to take out whips and beat them without mercy. This made Hairan even angrier. As he was about to attack, a few men were headed in his direction. It seemed he would run away because that was his usual reaction. But he didn't.

Hairan stood firm and fearless. He vowed to himself that he would never fear again. Hairan ran towards them angrily. The humans had strange things in their hands, which they aimed at Hairan. He was hit and temporarily became unconscious. After a while, he woke up to find himself with a chain around his neck.

Hairan tried to get out, but he could not. The humans beat him with their whips, but it only made him even angrier. He was furious. The animals around him watched in anticipation.

After trying to fight back, Hairan finally gave up. He walked weakly as all the animals stared at him. The humans put him in front of several rings of fires, each higher than the last. But he didn't go ahead. The humans beat him furiously and hollered at him, but he didn't move an inch. Then, out of nowhere, he furiously jumped through the rings while the humans still held on. Hairan miraculously remained untouched as the humans got injured by his force. The rings fell over, setting the entire place on fire.

The humans were so focused on trying to put out the fire that they forgot about the animals. Hairan took the chance and set them free. They thanked him as they ran off into the wild. However, his job wasn't done. "Help!" a voice shouted. He saw a creature tied onto one of the poles. He quickly yanked at its chain with all his force, which caused the chain to break. The animal was now free. He helped it walk through the thick smoke and led it to the jungle. He then lay down on the dirt exhausted. Suddenly, he saw the creature he had saved from the fire.

It was a female lioness-like creature, but she was sandy brown and white and was covered in cinnamon stripes. Her eyes were a deep ocean blue. Her voice was soft and gentle. But the creature's reaction was less peaceful than his.

"What do you want with me, strange creature?"asked the striped lioness.

"I'm strange? If anyone's strange, it's you. Is that how you react when someone saves you?" replied Hairan.

"Who are you and what do you want with me?" she asked.

"Look, I don't want to hurt you," he answered calmly. As she tried to get up, she yowled loudly.

"Is something wrong? Hairan asked.

"The humans beat me so much that my leg hurts when I walk," she replied. Hairan instantly ran up to her as he tried to help her walk. She then growled, asking, "What are you doing?"

"Relax, I'm trying to help you," replied Hairan.

"Can I trust you?" she asked.

"You'll have no chance out here in the wild with a bad leg. So, either way, you'll have to face me or random animals," said Hairan. She then tried to bite Hairan as he backed away. "What's wrong with you?" he asked.

"Leave me alone!"she said furiously.

"Fine then," said Hairan as he left her. As he slowly walked away, she then realized that the lion was right.

"Wait!"she shouted. "Please help me! But if you're up to any tricks, I'll fight you," she added.

Hairan turned back and helped her search for somewhere to rest. They finally found a cave and they both rested. Hairan said, "So, who are you?" She replied, "I'm Indira, the golden tigress. And you?"

"I'm Hairan, the black lion," he answered.

"I can see why your parents named you that. But why did you save me?" Indira asked, becoming suspicious again.

"I felt sorry for how those humans were treating you and those other animals," he replied.

"But how were you so brave? Weren't you scared?" she asked.

"Well, I once feared the humans. But if you fear, you let them control your lives," he replied. They then fell asleep.

It was dawn. The cool breeze blew across Hairan's face and he decided to go hunting while Indira was resting. Not too long after, he came back with a scrumptious breakfast of hare. By that time, Indira was awake and happy to have a fresh meal. She then thanked Hairan for saving her and the other animals. Soon, a week had passed. Hairan had taken care of her well. Her leg had healed, and she could run now. They had become great friends and now Indira wanted to repay Hairan. While they were walking, Indira said, "I am very grateful for all you have done for me. I really want to repay you."

"Well, there is one thing you can do for me. I want to go to the Gir Forest, but I don't know the way. I was wondering if you could guide me there," Hairan said.

"Yes, I know where it is. I was born there. But it's far away and many dangers await you," Indira answered.

"Well, I'm willing to take the risks," said Hairan.

"Okay, we can leave in a few days," said Indira. They planned the journey together. Upon second thought, Indira said, "We can leave tomorrow morning." Hairan was very happy to have such a great companion. The next day, they happily set out on their journey. On the way, Indira said, "We have to find the Blue River. By following the banks, it will lead us to the Gir Forest."

"But how do we find it?" asked Hairan.

"We have to find the cliff with the cedar tree growing at its side.

It will be a shortcut," said Indira. They walked through the terrain searching for a cliff. Since they were on a mountain, cliffs were in every corner. Hoping to find the cliff quicker, Hairan and Indira split up. However, they were unaware of the consequences it would bring.

It was near sunset. The creatures of the jungle prepared to rest as the danger started to arise. Indira lay beneath a large tree after tireless searching. She began to worry. She knew the dangers along the Gir Forest. She was worried Hairan would be unprepared for it. That was when she remembered that horrible day. Indira and her brother were just a few months old. They were going to see their mother, Rani, hunt. Everything seemed as usual. The birds were perched in the tall, lush trees lining the lane to the meadow. They had just begun to sing. The rabbits scampered through the thick green grass. The stream beside the road was full of swans gracefully swimming. It was the usual summer morning in the Gir Forest. But one noise disrupted the peacefulness—the sound of an elephant trumpeting angrily broke the peace. "Who is that elephant? He seems different from the others. Why is he so angry and mean?" asked Indira.

"Well, he thinks he should be king of the Gir Forest. He is a wicked creature who destroys anything in his sight. His herd pushed him out for his behavior," said Rani.

"Who is the true king of the Gir Forest?" asked Indira.

"There are many kings. One lion rules over an area of the forest. However, each is a descendant of the Great Lion, the one who founded the Gir Forest," replied Rani. After walking for a few minutes, they finally reached the end of the trail, which brought them to the meadow. Chital and various types of prey were right in front of them. The cubs watched in excitement as their mother chose a target. A lone chital doe was by the stream taking a sip of water. Rani quietly stalked her.

"One of the most important rules of hunting is when to attack. You must slowly and carefully stalk your prey until you're close enough to pounce on it. Before you pounce, stay still for a moment, and when the prey is vulnerable, you pounce!" said Rani. The cubs nodded their heads and Rani slowly crept towards the doe. She made sure that she was as quiet as she could be, and she calculated her every move. But sometimes, great hunters fail.

The doe was smart and experienced. She had noticed the tigress. It would be easy to spot her, though. Rani was a white tigress, and she couldn't camouflage herself in the tall, dry, brown grass. The doe ran away, alerting the other animals. Rani ran as fast as she could, trying to get a grip on the doe, but she failed. The meadow was now empty, and the tigers were hungry. Disappointed, they decided to settle for a rabbit. But it seemed they wouldn't need to. A large figure stood in the shadows. The cubs hid behind their mother's back in fear, but Rani seemed calm. Suddenly, a tiger stepped out. But he wasn't an ordinary tiger. He was a golden tiger. He had dark brown fur and taupe stripes. His eyes were a deep blue. Rani and the tiger nuzzled. The cubs were even more scared.

"It's okay. He won't hurt you. You can come out now," said Rani.

Indira went first, staring at the huge tiger. She was the size of his paw. She nervously asked, "Who are you?"

"I'm Rajah, your father. You and your brother seem hungry. Would you like me to hunt for you?" the tiger asked. The cubs nodded their heads. He hunted a chital for them and stayed a while. He headed back into the forest to continue to patrol his territory. Rani and the cubs ate their fill and prepared to head back to the den. But that was when it happened. The elephant was heading towards them. His heavy footsteps shook the ground. Rani and the cubs tried to hide in the bushes but were spotted. The angry elephant chased them through the forest. Rani roared, trying to call for help. Luckily, Rajah was in the area. He followed her voice and found her and the cubs cornered by a large boulder.

The elephant smiled evilly and prepared to stomp on them. Rani hugged her cubs tightly. Then Rajah jumped onto the elephant's back, distracting him temporarily. "Run! Get out of here!" shouted Rajah.

They ran back to the den with tears in their eyes and huddled in the corner. When it was night and the cubs were fast asleep, Rani went to the boulder to see if Rajah was safe. She then heard loud noises and saw red and blue lights, along with humans. Rajah was nowhere in sight. When she tried to turn back, the humans captured her and took her away. Early in the morning, the cubs woke up to see their mother gone. Indira, as the eldest, decided to go look for her, and she told her brother to stay back at the den. She followed her mother's scent, which led her outside of the Gir Forest. Soon, the scent was erased, and she was now lost in the jungle. She cried all day, but no one answered her. She roamed the jungles, only getting into deeper danger. The humans from the tent had found and captured her. That was the most horrible day of her entire life. She remembered that day so clearly that it made her cry.

Her thoughts were interrupted when a group of birds flew overhead. She wondered if Hairan was experienced enough to go on the journey. She heard about of all the adventures he and Deepa had gone on, but it seemed he over exaggerated it. Was he truly ready for true danger?

She got up and stared at the sky. It was getting late, and she didn't find anything. Indira began to wonder if Hairan had found anything. That was when she noticed something. She saw a huge cedar sticking out of the side of a cliff. She quickly ran towards it. Indira instantly recognized it. It was the cliff she was looking for!

She roared for Hairan. While she waited, she decided to look at Blue River. Suddenly, the edge of the cliff where she stood broke off. Before she could run back, she fell into the river. Hairan had already noticed her and was trying to alert her. As he tried to grab hold of her, he went tumbling as well. As they fell into the raging waters, Indira struggled to swim. But after all he had gone through, Hairan had learned how to swim through strong currents. He dragged Indira to dry land, swimming with all his might. Hairan rested on the shore for a moment to regain his strength. He turned to Indira who was heavily panting. She shook herself dry and said in shock, "How did you do that?"

"Do what?" asked Hairan.

"How could you swim through a raging river and get to the shore?" asked Indira.

"I've learned a lot from the wilderness, and I know how to get out of most situations," he replied.

"Well, thank you again for saving me," said Indira happily. She was surprised by Hairan. He seemed more experienced than her. Perhaps they would make it to the Gir Forest. They continued to walk along the riverbank. The evening sun started to disappear, and the moon started to rise. They searched for shelter near the river. "I found a place to rest!" shouted Indira.

Hairan went beside her and asked, "What are you talking about?"

"Don't you see? We can take shelter beneath that giant tree," said Indira.

"That? We can't go there. We have to find a cave or somewhere that looks a little more stable," said Hairan.

"I'm sure the roots are stable. Anyway, if a tiger can live in there, I'm sure a lion can," said Indira. She chuckled as she quickly slid beneath the tree. Hairan followed behind, roughly slipping into the space. When he went inside, he was surprised. It was spacious but very dark.

"Aren't you worried that you could be unaware of something coming up to you? It's so dark in here that I can't even see my own paws," complained Hairan.

"Well, you should be grateful for what you have. Not everything in your life will be like how you planned it," said Indira.

Hairan remained silent as he thought about her words. He turned to see Indira staring at the moon sadly as if she was remembering something.

"Are you okay?" asked Hairan as Indira shook her head to get out of her trance.

"I'm fine," said Indira. They fell asleep whilst planning for the next day. At dawn, they set out on their journey.

"So, where do we go next?" asked Hairan.

"We have to follow the riverbanks for another day," replied Indira. As she walked further down the banks, she was surprised. Indira saw wild berry patches of all kinds right in front of her. The entire shore and jungle were covered by them. The only place they didn't grow was where the trees were. Indira excitedly ran towards them as she jumped around.

"What's so exciting about plants?" asked Hairan.

"These aren't any ordinary plants. They're berry plants! Haven't you ever tried berries?" asked Indira. Hairan shook his head. "Well, they're the greatest food in the world! Even better than chital!" exclaimed Indira.

Hairan tried a berry, worrying what would happen. As soon as he ate it, he gobbled up the rest. "You're right! This is the greatest food in the world!" said Hairan. They ate the berries until they couldn't eat anymore. Afternoon came. Indira and Hairan lay down, tired and full, in the sun. But it wasn't over yet. Indira noticed a glimmering silver thing leap into the river. It was a fish. She got up, shouting, "A fish! I haven't had one of those in a long time!" Hairan got up and asked, "Would you like me to catch a few?" Indira nodded as she watched him. He quickly pounced into the water but caught none. "That's not the way to do it," said Indira.

"Can you teach me then?" asked Hairan.

"Of course, I can," she said. She led him to a small multi-step waterfall, more ahead of the river. "Watch me," she said, standing by the edge of the water. A fish leaped down the waterfall, straight into Indira's mouth. While she ate, Hairan tried. He failed at first but caught one the second time. But since they were distracted, danger could easily catch them. They ran along the riverbanks, chasing each other like cubs.

While they were swimming in the river, a shady figure was heading towards them. Indira barely glanced at it, thinking it was a log. She then looked back to see a crocodile heading towards them. "Hairan! There's a crocodile behind you!" said Indira. They quickly ran back to the shore and farther down, near to the river's end. They shook themselves dry and laughed.

"That was an exciting yet scary day! I'll never forget it," said Hairan.

"That was extremely close. We have to be more careful next time," said Indira. She was once again reminded of the jungle's dangers. They quickly fell asleep in a cave by the shore, tired from all the excitement.

At dawn, they continued on their journey. Indira and Hairan were excited since they would reach the Gir Forest within three days. They were heading towards Shady Forest, which had tall trees that hardly let in sunlight. In the forest, there was a tree that rivaled the rest. It was huge and taller than all the other trees. It was called the Giant Banyan. It was visible from far away. Indira and Hairan sat at the river's edge, staring off into the horizon. "What are you looking for?" asked Hairan.

"I'm looking for the Giant Banyan. It seems I can't see it yet," replied Indira. All she could see was a thick green canopy along the horizon. Millions of trees made up the canopy. How would they spot the single banyan? Indira was tired of straining her eyes and decided to go up a hill. She ran into the jungle and looked for a high place. She saw one of the hills and went up. She saw a tree with a large, tall trunk covered with thick foliage. It was so majestic and beautiful from far away. It seemed to be the tree they were looking for. They went towards it excitedly running. After a while, they noticed that some of its flowers and seed pods spotted the grass, which was a sign they were close.

Since they were tired, they quickly slurped up some water from a stream. Indira could see the tree right ahead. She and Hairan ran with their remaining strength and rested by the tree. They were in shock. The tree was so tall that they felt like ants in its sight. It was shady and dark. Not a single beam of sunlight got through its lush leaves. They decided to lie down under the tree to rest.

"Wow. The places along the way to the Gir Forest are so beautiful. I wonder what it's like. I'm so excited and it's still early. Can we rest for an hour and continue on to the next location?" asked Hairan.

"Of course, we can," said Indira.

"So, where do we go from here?" asked Hairan.

"We have to go through Peacock Caverns," replied Indira.

"Peacock Caverns? What's that?" asked Hairan.

"It's a tunnel that leads to the next location, which will take us to the Gir Forest. Peacocks live in the area, giving it the name," she replied.

"So, how do we find Peacock Caverns?" asked Hairan.

"There's supposed to be some jungle path that will lead us straight to it. But it's hidden away," said Indira.

As they went deeper into Shady Forest, they encountered many obstacles. The terrain was very rough and rocky. It was easy to get injured. Venomous snakes hid throughout the forest looking for prey. Indira and Hairan were very scared. They wanted to leave the forest as soon as possible. They ran with all their speed, leaping over obstacles without resting. But that would lead them into more danger. Hairan decided to take a quick sip of water while Indira continued to run ahead. They were near the end of Shady Forest. That was when Indira's foot got trapped beneath a tree root.

Indira struggled to pull her foot out. Since she was focused on trying to get her foot out, she was unaware that a snake was coiled up in the tree and was about to attack her. But Indira heard the snake's hiss and tried to back away. She yowled for Hairan in fright. The snake's mouth opened wide to bite her. As it was about to attack her, Hairan jumped and slapped it to the ground. The snake slithered away in fear. Hairan helped Indira get her foot out, and they quickly tried to get through the forest to look for the trail.

After a tedious amount of time, the sun began to set, and they still hadn't gotten anywhere. They then decided to find somewhere to rest and would continue searching tomorrow. "Are you sure we're going to find Peacock Caverns? We are so close to the Gir Forest. We have to find it soon," said Hairan worriedly.

"Relax; I'm sure we'll find it by tomorrow," she replied. Suddenly, fire and voices appeared right ahead of them. They hid in the bushes as they watched. There were humans that seemed to be searching for something.

"What if they're looking for Peacock Caverns?" said Hairan.

"They could be looking for Peacock Caverns. But at the same time, they could be looking for something else. It's almost night and there will be lots of things out there," commented Indira.

"Come on, Indira. Please?" begged Hairan. She sighed as they quietly followed the humans. They followed the humans, but they still didn't see anything.

"Are you sure we should continue following them? We still didn't reach the caverns and we could get caught any moment," reasoned Indira.

"We should be patient. Just a while longer and then we'll leave. Okay?" said Hairan. Indira remained silent as she continued to watch the humans with suspicious eyes. Suddenly, the humans stopped and shouted joyfully. Hairan and Indira looked ahead to see a tunnel. They were astonished and they knew they had found Peacock Caverns.

"I think this is Peacock Caverns. But how are we going to get through the people?" asked Indira.

Hairan walked out of the bushes. Before he could do anything, the humans flashed a light at him and then ran away. The animals sensed that the humans were not hunters but were scared. They quickly headed for the caverns. A small doorway was visible from across the tunnel. They ran towards it in excitement, wondering what sights they would see. Suddenly, they stopped. As they entered the room, they saw various tiles on the ground with different depictions.

"Wait!" said Hairan, stopping Indira from crossing. "I think this is some kind of puzzle. You will have to step on certain tiles. If you don't, something will happen."

"Well, we can't read any of this. So, what will we do now?" asked Indira.

"We'll have to try to leap over it," answered Hairan. "You try first. You're more agile than me," added Hairan.

Indira nodded as she quickly leaped over the tiles. She made it to the other side safely. Hairan was nervous. He had never jumped so far. He was motivated by the memories he made on the journey. The leap was nothing compared to what he had already gone through. He leaped in midair, closing his eyes. He looked to see that he had made it. But then he turned around. When he jumped, he had kicked a small rock onto one of the tiles. A rumble started to echo through the tunnel. Hairan and Indira stared ahead in fear. A gigantic boulder was rolling towards them! They ran as fast as they could, trying to escape the boulder. But it gained on them each second. Soon, the boulder was right behind their tails and there was no way out! The boulder had chased them to a dead end! At the last moment, Hairan finally thought of a plan.

"Climb up the wall!" shouted Hairan. The wall was unusually bumpy, and if climbed, it would hold them long enough until the boulder crashed. Hairan's plan was successful. The boulder crashed into the wall and they landed right on top of it. As they entered the next room, they carefully investigated it after their experience. It seemed to be safe. Hairan went inside first. The room was covered in torches. As Hairan went in deeper, he saw two lanes. He called Indira, saying, "This place seems safe. But now there are two pathways ahead. What should we do?"

"I think we should explore them. Let's split up," said Indira. When they went down the paths, the paths led to more and more paths. They quickly ran out to the room, worried they would get lost.

"Each path leads to more paths. I don't know what to do," said Indira. Hairan froze for a second as he sniffed the ground. "What is it?" asked Indira.

"I think I know how to get out of here," said Hairan. He had realized that certain pathways had burnt torches and ash along them. The path Indira went into had nothing. He supposed that the ash would lead them out since they were a sign of humans. They went from path to path to investigate them. After looking around, they followed the scent of animals and humans, and they also saw pieces of freshly burnt firewood. They followed that path, and it led them straight out. With contented hearts, they had their fill of food and slept.

Dawn came. They got up early with excitement. They knew this would be the last day until their final destination. Their hearts pounded with anticipation. They would finally have true freedom. They could live life worry free for the Gir Forest was a sanctuary for all animals. The only thing separating them from it was the expansive White Desert. It stretched far beyond the horizon, and it would be very difficult to cross since trees were rare in the desert, and the heat of the scorching sun would dehydrate them quickly. Water was also very scarce, but they were determined to continue on. They followed the sandy areas of the jungle, which would lead them to the desert.

After walking for a while, they saw the White Desert. They watched in amazement from a pasture of dry grass. "Wow! It's so beautiful!" said Hairan. "It reminds me of Africa. Except there, we had normal sand." They slid down the slope of sand as they walked further. Since they were tired and hot, they decided to look for shelter. They saw a small pond near a palm grove. They decided to rest there. Soon, night crept in slowly. The starry sky and the moon shone brightly. The whole place was lit up beautifully and there were fireflies all around. It was as if they were competing with the stars.

The cool night breeze ruffled their fur. It was such a serene and peaceful place. "This place is even more beautiful at night!" said Hairan.

"I agree. Tomorrow, we'll start our journey before dawn, since it will be very hot, and we'll get tired quickly. We'll head south to the end of the desert. At its edge, we'll find a pathway that leads directly into the Gir Forest," said Indira. They fell asleep peacefully, knowing that their journey was finally going to end.

Chapter 8

The Journey's End

When they woke up the next day, they were too excited to eat. "We're leaving now!" said Hairan.

"What? Don't you want to hunt before continuing?" asked Indira.

"I just have to go. We'll reach it earlier if we leave now. Come on!" said Hairan. Indira sighed, shaking her head. They then ran as fast as they could through the desert. As the day went on and the afternoon sun came, the heat began to have an effect on them and they were very thirsty. They were feeling weak, but they were determined to go on. Luckily, they were at the desert's edge, and they could see lush green grass ahead. They crawled with their remaining strength. They barely made it into the shade and were now very weak. They needed water quickly, but they couldn't even move now. They were about to collapse when an unexpected ray of hope came.

They heard gentle footsteps coming towards them. It was a human. They tried to hide but they could not. They were so weak from dehydration that they didn't have the strength to move. When they were about to faint, they got a glimpse of the human approaching them. They were sure that it would be the end. But to their surprise, the lady was kind to them. She threw some water on the ground and on their bodies and they drank it up instantly. After lapping up the water, the lady gave them something to eat.

They hungrily devoured it and then began to feel drowsy and fell fast asleep.

A few hours later, they woke up and were shocked to find themselves in the Gir Forest. It seemed as if the kind lady must have taken them there. "How did we get here?" said Hairan.

"The lady, she was actually good to us. We would've died if she didn't help us. Some humans are very kind," said Indira. They excitedly ran around the Gir Forest, finally having peace of mind.

"I can't believe this. We're finally here. It truly is beautiful. I just wish my aunt would be able to see this," said Hairan. His smile turned into a frown.

"Well, why don't we continue to explore the Gir Forest? This is barely a glimpse of it," said Indira, who hoped to take his mind off his troubles. They walked through the forest. Even after all the beautiful places Hairan had encountered, none were like the Gir Forest. The land was mountainous and rocky. A beautiful emerald-green river ran through the area, and tall reeds grew by its banks. The entire region around the river was covered with bushes and tall, lush trees. It was cool since the trees formed a canopy by the edge of the water. Other parts were savannah-like, with small shady trees and thick dry grass. Most of the Gir Forest consisted of meadows lined with thick, luscious trees and wild berries. Hairan was so amazed by its beauty. It was worth all the trouble to get there.

That was when Hairan realized the lessons he had learned from the journey. The greatest lessons he had learned were that family is your greatest treasure, and freedom is worth fighting for. With perseverance, courage, and strength, he had made it.

Indira and Hairan lay beside the riverbank, in the green grass beneath a tall, lush tree. The fresh dew on their fur cooled them down, along with the breeze that blew across the river. "It was worth everything to come here. If only my pack and Aunt Deepa were here. They would've loved it here," said Hairan. Indira nuzzled him and said, "Well, they'll always be with you in your heart, and you have me at least."

"You're right. I did learn important lessons from the journey. If I hadn't left my pack, I wouldn't have met my aunt Deepa, which means I never would've gone on this journey. If I hadn't lost her, I wouldn't have learned my lesson and I never would've met you. You're such a wonderful friend," said Hairan. Suddenly, strange sounds caught Hairan's attention. "It must be my imagination," he said in his head.

"Hairan? Is someone calling for you?" asked Indira.

He realized that someone was really calling for him. "Hello?" said Hairan. Shady figures stood between the shadowy trees. He began to growl as they approached him. Hairan froze in shock. A lioness and a pack of jackals stared at him with tears in their eyes. The lioness was Deepa, and the jackals were Hairan's pack. "Aunt Deepa?" asked Hairan.

"Hairan! You made it!" she shouted.

Hairan suddenly backed away. "I'm sorry. I'm sorry for leaving you. I'm sorry for acting like a burden since I found out the truth about my mother. Ever since I lost you, I realized something. You were with me through my entire journey. You nearly sacrificed your life with my risky plans. Ever since I started the journey, I've been looking for my mother. But now, I realize my mother was always beside me. You were my mother along the way!"

"Come here, Hairan," said Deepa as they hugged. "But I'm not the only one here," she added.

Hairan then ran to his pack and hugged them tightly, saying, "I'm sorry for leaving the pack without telling you. When Musafa told me the truth, I was so upset."

Zahara interrupted him as she said, "We understand. We should've told you the truth. I'm just glad to have you back again."

"But how did you reach here?" asked Hairan, laughing.

Jabari replied, "We heard that you went to the Gir Forest, and we went on a quest to find you. But when we arrived, we kept roaming all over, searching for you. Finally, we picked up your scent and it led us here."

"You did all of this for me?" asked Hairan.

"Well, you're our son," replied Jabari.

Hairan then introduced Indira to his pack and to Deepa. They were glad to have a new pack member. They sang and danced for joy to celebrate Hairan's return. They walked down the dirt road to the center of the Gir Forest to hunt some food to celebrate. It was decorated with blue and red flowers beneath towering trees covered in vines. Hairan smiled as he lifted his head up high. He watched his family and his pack. He ran ahead with a smile on his face, and he truly had a feeling of belonging. He had the happiest life a lion could have. Now, he would start a new life in the Gir Forest, full of joy and wonder.